OSLO...

or

The Whale Whose Tail Looked a Bit Like a Wellington Boot

Stephen Bench-Capon

First published in Great Britain as a softback original in 2021

Copyright © Stephen Bench-Capon

The moral right of this author has been asserted.

Typeset in New Century Schoolbook LT Std

Cover illustration by Juana Maria Muschietti.

Design, typesetting and publishing by UK Book Publishing

www.ukbookpublishing.com

ISBN: 978-1-914195-85-3

For David and Natalie.

Acknowledgements

I want to say thank you to Mike and Mum for reading drafts and giving intelligent input, to Juan for his support, to Juana for the cover illustration, to Christian and Lisann for their words of encouragement, to Christine for her proofreading, to James for writing the blurb, to the team at UK Book Publishing for their help and finally to Eka, simply for making this and everything else I do possible. Thank you.

About the Author

Stephen Bench-Capon grew up on the Wirral in England and moved to Germany in 2009 after graduating in Modern and Medieval Languages from Cambridge University. He currently lives in Berlin with his wife and two children.

Stephen has always enjoyed writing in various formats, both as a hobby and professionally. *Oslo or The Whale Whose Tail Looked a Bit Like a Wellington Boot* is Stephen's first published work of fiction.

Stephen can be contacted via email at *herrbench@outlook.com* or on Twitter *@herrbench*.

Oslo...

O slo was two. He hadn't always been two. He used to be one and before that he'd even been zero – when he'd been very young. He didn't remember anything about that, but his dad sometimes mentioned it.

Oslo's dad was quite a lot older than Oslo. Oslo didn't know how old exactly, maybe eleven or twenty-two or even thirty, although probably not thirty, because that would have been very old for a whale. He was definitely older than two though. And a lot bigger than Oslo.

So Oslo and his dad weren't the same age or the same size, but they did have some things in common. They were both whales, to start with. And they both liked krill and ketchup.

Oslo's dad said he liked mayonnaise – he said he was quite continental – but he generally ate some of Oslo's ketchup whenever Oslo was having ketchup. So Oslo was pretty sure his dad liked ketchup.

Oslo wasn't very continental. He didn't even really know what being continental was supposed to mean, to be honest. But he didn't like mayonnaise anyway. It didn't matter though. He just didn't eat any mayonnaise anyway. And that was fine.

Oslo liked being two. And Oslo liked his dad, too. He liked the way they did things together that he liked doing. Like swimming and blowing water out of his blowhole and eating krill and ketchup. Always in that order, of course. You couldn't go swimming and blowing water out of your blowhole after eating krill and ketchup. Every young whale knew that because every dad whale told them about it. Oslo's dad had told Oslo maybe ten or even eleven times not to do anything complicated after eating.

"Just sit around for a bit," his dad would say –- which Oslo thought was fine because he liked it when his tummy wasn't hurting.

Oslo's mum wasn't there. Normally, mum whales look after their children, but Oslo's mum didn't because she wasn't there. That's why his dad did it. Oslo's dad said sometimes,

"She just went off."

Oslo didn't really know what that meant. He knew mayonnaise could go off if you left it out of the fridge for too long. He didn't really mind that because he didn't eat mayonnaise even when it had been left in the fridge for a long time and even when it hadn't gone off. But he'd never been in a fridge and he hadn't gone off. Not as far as he could tell anyway. So he didn't see why his mum would've gone off. Unless she was made of mayonnaise, but that didn't seem very likely.

His dad didn't really like talking about it though. Dads didn't seem to really like talking about mums going off, it seemed. So Oslo didn't ask about it very often. Oslo didn't like making his dad talk about things his dad didn't like talking about. So Oslo normally asked his dad other things. Like where ketchup comes from. His dad liked talking about things like that and would smile and say funny words like 'tomatoes'.

SCHOOLS

Some people think that only fish go to school. And some very clever people, who have been paying attention at their school, will tell you that whales are not actually fish. They are something called mammals. That is true enough, but it doesn't stop them going to school. Most mammals go to school. Even platypuses go to school, though it isn't quite clear if anyone really knows whether they're mammals or not, however much they've been paying attention at their school.

Anyway, whales definitely go to school. In fact, whales go to school when they're just three years old, because they're already so big when they're three years old that if they waited any longer, there wouldn't be enough room in the whale classroom for the whale class. And if you can't fit the class in the classroom, then it's really just a room. And if you've just got lots of rooms and haven't got any classrooms, then it isn't really a school, and then there isn't much point in going there.

After Oslo had finished being two, he was three. And because he was still a whale, that meant he started going to school, because whales go to school when they're three years old.

TEACHERS

One thing Oslo learned after going to school for a bit was that teachers seemed to know most things. The main thing they liked doing seemed to be telling you lots of things you didn't know. Without anyone even asking or anything. They'd just start talking about where krill comes from or how oxygen works or why it sometimes rains even though really the water is full of water anyway. On top of this, teachers could answer questions. You could just ask them something and they'd tell you the answer.

Oslo's dad did that as well sometimes, though he often seemed a bit drowsy and just said something like, "That's a great question, Oslo. I'll think about it and tell you the answer in the morning." And thinking about it, Oslo realised that he'd often forgotten by the morning that his dad was supposed to be thinking about it and telling him in the morning. He'd ask his dad about that this evening. If he didn't forget.

Oslo's teacher was quite different. She wasn't drowsy. She was very bubbly and always knew the answer to everything. Even when the answer had very complicated sounding words in it like 'photosynthesis' or 'pulmonary'.

One day, Oslo decided to ask his teacher a question that he'd wanted to know the answer to pretty much ever since he'd started school.

"Miss?"

"Yes, Oslo?"

"Why does everyone at school call me 'Wellington'?"

"Not everyone calls you 'Wellington', Oslo."

"Well, no, Miss. You just called me 'Oslo', Miss. But most of the children call me 'Wellington'."

"Well, yes."

"So why?"

"Well,..."

Oslo's teacher had quite a long think at this point. She didn't normally think this long about the answers to questions. Oslo was just starting to think that maybe she seemed a bit drowsy when she answered.

"Well, it's because of your tail, Oslo."

"It's because of my tail, Miss?"

"Yes, it's because of your tail, Oslo."

Now it was Oslo's turn to think. He thought for a long time, too. Well, a long time for a young whale anyway. Then he spoke again.

"Miss?"

"Yes, Oslo?"

"I don't understand, Miss."

"Well, your tail, Oslo, well, it kind of looks ... you could say, a little bit, I suppose some of the children think it maybe almost looks a bit like ... well, a bit like a wellington boot."

Oslo looked at his tail and thought again. This time he thought for an even longer time for a young whale. And he thought that yes, his tail, it did kind of look ... you could say, a little bit, he did suppose, he did think it maybe almost looked a bit like ... well, a bit like a wellington boot.

Oslo did a bit more thinking. He'd definitely have to take some time off thinking that evening. Now he was even thinking too much about thinking too much. What he didn't realise was that, while he was thinking, he kept saying – very quietly but he was saying it – he kept saying 'Wellington, Wellington, Wellington, Wellington!' to himself, over and over.

"Wellington, Wellington, Wellington, Wellington."

After about two minutes, his teacher thought she should say something. She didn't know quite what to say but she thought she should say something. And as she had spent the last two minutes listening to someone saying 'Wellington, Wellington, Wellington, Wellington' over and over, it was little surprise that when she did say something she ended up saying,

"Wellington?" And then Oslo said,

"Yes!"

But it wasn't a little 'yes?' with a question mark, like he was asking 'yes, what would you like to say to me?' It was a 'Yes!' with a big, confident exclamation mark. He repeated,

"Yes! Wellington! I'm Wellington!"

The teacher was definitely getting unusually drowsy and even a bit muddled now. She seemed to have lost most of her bubbliness so, as Oslo proudly swam off, she just repeated,

"Wellington?"

Except her 'Wellington' was quite a muddled 'Wellington' and definitely had a big question mark after it.

Then, alone in the classroom, Oslo's teacher didn't realise it either, but while she was thinking, she kept saying – very quietly but she was saying it – she kept saying 'Wellington, Wellington, Wellington,

Wellington' to herself, over and over, for about two minutes. Then the school bell rang, and she swam off, because if she hadn't, she would have been late for home time.

CRYING

*T*here are lots of reasons to cry. The most obvious ones are when something hurts – when you conk your head on something – or when you're sad – when you lose something, or someone's mean to you.

But you can also cry when you're cross, when you're disappointed or when you're sorry.

One reason to cry is when something unusual happens. You might feel happy and sad and relieved and surprised all at the same time, and then it's all so complicated. And you're often quite tired too and then it's all so confusing that you just don't know what to do and you start to cry.

That's what had happened to Oslo's dad when Oslo had been born. He'd cried. He'd

been happy because Oslo was there. He'd
been sad because Oslo's mum was struggling.
He'd been relieved because Oslo was healthy.
He'd been surprised because Oslo's tail looked
a bit like a wellington boot. And he'd been
tired because grown-ups are often tired when
children are born. And he'd started to cry.

Oslo's dad had known about his tail since
Oslo had started being born because the
whale's tail is the first thing you see when a
whale is born.

Oslo's dad hadn't seen a lot of whales being
born but he had seen lots of whales after
they'd been born, and he realised that Oslo's
tail was a bit different from the other whales'
tails. It was the only whale's tail he'd seen that
looked a bit like a wellington boot. He'd been
a bit surprised to begin with. But the doctors
had said that it was perfectly healthy and was
nothing to worry about. It just looked a bit like
a wellington boot. That was all. He'd never
talked to Oslo about it though. Oslo had never
asked about it and he'd never really thought it

had been important enough to talk about.

Oslo's dad was more than just a little surprised when Oslo came home from school that day and replied to his usual 'Hello, Oslo' with,

"Wellington! I'm Wellington!"

"Wellington? You're Wellington?"

Oslo's dad understood the connection between the shape of Oslo's tail and the name, but he was a little confused by his son's enthusiasm.

"Why didn't you tell me before about my tail?" asked Oslo.

"Well, it's just a tail that happens to look a bit like a wellington boot. That's all. What should I have told you about it?" asked his dad.

"But I never realised! I mean, I hardly ever look at my tail, it's not easy to bend my neck that way – and the whole time it's been looking like a wellington boot!"

"Well, it doesn't matter – I didn't think that there was any reason to talk about it."

"But it's my tail!"

"Yes, but it's perfectly healthy and it's nothing to worry about. It's just not really quite the way a tail's supposed to be, that's all."

"What do you mean 'supposed to be'? I'm me and I'm supposed to be me!"

"Oh, Oslo," he began.

"Wellington!" replied Oslo, interrupting him.

"You really want me to call you 'Wellington'?"

"Yes!"

There it was again: the same big, confident 'Yes!' with an exclamation mark that Oslo had said to his teacher earlier that afternoon. And there it was again, too: that mixture of happy, sad, relieved, surprised feelings that Oslo's dad had felt when Oslo had been born. And he was a bit tired.

Oslo's dad noticed that his cheek was a bit wet. But it wasn't the normal wet from the normal water that whales are normally swimming around in anyway. There was a tear on his face. He was crying.

From now on, Oslo's dad was going to call him 'Wellington'.

NAMES

In most cases, the parents decide on the name of their child. Normally, they talk about it and think about it and first decide on lots of names they don't like before eventually deciding on a name they do like. And that's the name they call their child.

And in most cases, the child likes the name too because it gets called it all the time and, of course, because in most cases the parents have chosen a very good name to begin with.

That's how it was with Wellington. His dad had always called him 'Oslo' and he had always liked the name 'Oslo'. His case had just stopped being like most cases when the other children had started calling him 'Wellington'. It didn't mean he didn't like the name 'Oslo' anymore, but it did mean that it was a bit more complicated than it had been before people had started calling him 'Wellington'.

Wellington wasn't the only whale with a slightly complicated naming situation. There was another whale at school whose name was really 'Leo', but who was often called 'Swimmy', because he liked swimming, and because some people thought 'Leo' was a slightly unusual name for a whale. Wellington thought that almost all whales quite liked swimming, so this wasn't a very good reason just to call this one particular whale 'Swimmy'. But Leo didn't seem to mind. He thought 'Swimmy' was quite a good name for someone who liked swimming. And people did sometimes call him 'Leo'. Just sometimes 'Swimmy' as well.

Wellington wanted to do things differently. Having decided to be called 'Wellington', he was determined that everyone should call him 'Wellington'. The three main groups of people were: children, grown-ups and his dad. His dad was a grown-up, of course, but he was such a special grown-up, Wellington decided to give him his own group.

Giving his dad his own group also meant that one whole group was taken care of already. His dad had already agreed to call Wellington 'Wellington', so that meant there were just two more groups to go.

The children were also fairly easy to convince. Most of them called Wellington 'Wellington' already, and all he had to do with the others was say, "Call me 'Wellington," when they called him 'Oslo'. And then they called him 'Wellington'.

The last group, grown-ups other than his dad, was the most complicated group. Grown-ups other than his dad were often complicated. He had already told one teacher that he wanted to be called 'Wellington', but now he had to tell all the others.

There were lots of other teachers for lots of other subjects at his school and Wellington didn't even know who they all were, so he had the good idea to tell the headteacher to tell the other teachers. As far as he understood, it was the headteacher's job to tell the other teachers what to do. So telling them one more thing that they had to do should be fairly doable.

Anyone who wanted to speak to the headteacher had to wait outside her office between 2 and 4 o'clock on Monday, Wednesday or Friday. As today was Monday, and Wellington was quite keen to be called 'Wellington' by everyone as soon as possible, he went along at 2 o'clock to wait to speak to the headteacher.

Luckily for Wellington, most people didn't really like speaking to the headteacher, so there was no-one else waiting outside her office, and he could swim right in.

"Name?" asked the headteacher.

Wellington hadn't spoken to the headteacher in her office before and he didn't realise that this was what she said to everyone who came to see her. So he was quite surprised that the headteacher seemed to have guessed exactly why he was here.

"Well, that's exactly why I'm here," Wellington said, which wasn't what the headteacher had been expecting at all. Normally when she said 'Name?' everyone just said what their name was.

"That's exactly why you're here?"

"Yes. Because my name is 'Wellington'. Or rather – well, yes – my name is 'Wellington'. Now. And I want all the grown-ups to call me 'Wellington'. And it's your job to tell all the grown-ups what to do. The teachers anyway, as I understand it. So I want to ask you to tell the teachers to call me 'Wellington'."

"So your name is 'Wellington'?"

"Yes. Wellington."

"And you want the teachers to call you 'Wellington'?"

"Yes. Wellington."

"Well, what do they call you now?"

"Oslo."

"Oslo?"

"Yes."

"Why 'Oslo'?"

The headteacher wasn't very good with names and faces so she never really bothered learning the names and faces of the children because she wouldn't have been very good with them anyway.

"Well, I used to be called 'Oslo'," said Wellington.

"But now you're called 'Wellington'?"

"Yes. Wellington."

"How did this happen?"

"I decided it."

"You decided to change your name to 'Wellington'?"

"Yes. Wellington."

"Can you just decide to change your name?"

The headteacher really didn't know the answer to her last question but Wellington seemed quite well informed, so he presumably knew, which was why she'd asked him.

"Yes. Wellington."

Wellington hoped if he said 'Yes. Wellington' enough, it would convince the headteacher to agree.

'Wellington' was his name after all. And it was a very good name too, Wellington thought.

"Wellington?"

"Yes. Wellington."

The headteacher noticed that Wellington's tail looked a bit like a wellington boot and was wondering if that had anything to do with the fact that his name was 'Wellington', but then she thought that that didn't really matter, so she asked one more time,

"Wellington?"

And Wellington answered one more time,

"Yes. Wellington."

And then the headteacher, who didn't really like causing problems, just said,

"OK, Wellington. I'll tell the other teachers to call you 'Wellington'."

"Thank you!" said Wellington, and he swam off, quite delighted with how his meeting with the headteacher had gone.

That Friday, in the headteacher's weekly notice to all teachers, which included news,

information and instructions, right at the
bottom, after various bits of news and
information, there was an instruction which
read:

INSTRUCTION TO ALL TEACHERS

THE WHALE WHO SAYS HIS NAME
IS 'WELLINGTON' IS TO BE CALLED
'WELLINGTON'.

When the headteacher sent an instruction
telling the other teachers to do something,
they usually did it. So after that, the whale
who said his name was 'Wellington' was called
'Wellington'. By the children, by his dad, and
by all the grown-ups who weren't his dad. By
everyone.

LEARNING

One of the things Wellington and the other children spent most of their time at school doing was learning. There were different kinds of learning.

The first kind of learning was learning new words like 'tributary' and 'Tokyo'. Wellington liked learning new words because it meant he didn't only have to use the words he already knew, like 'river' and 'city'. And he thought it was more interesting to be able to use lots of different words to describe things. Except for himself. For him, there was only one word which he wanted people to use: 'Wellington'.

Another kind of learning was learning how things worked. Wellington liked learning how things worked, things like the rain and the rivers, including tributaries, and the seas and the oceans. 'The water cycle', the geography teacher had called it, and it was very interesting.

Wellington's favourite kind of learning, however, wasn't learning new words or learning how things worked. It was learning to make connections between things. This didn't mean connections like the connections between rivers, like the confluences where a tributary meets the main river. This meant connections like humans wearing hats when it rains. Whales don't wear hats when it rains because they don't mind getting their heads wet but humans don't like getting their heads wet. So, when it rains, they wear hats to keep their heads dry.

Wellington liked making connections like this. Because normally if he connected things together, he could work out the answers to questions that started with 'why'. And the answers to the questions that started with 'why', were normally Wellington's favourite answers.

The names of things normally answered questions that started with 'what' and the way things worked normally answered questions that started with 'how'. These were good answers too, but not quite as good as answers to questions that started with 'why'.

So far, the question that started with 'why' that had interested Wellington most had been why the children at school called him 'Wellington'. He hadn't been able to work out the connection between his tail looking a bit like a wellington boot and the children calling him 'Wellington'. But his teacher had.

By now though, Wellington had been going to school for longer and had done lots of learning to make connections and had got quite good at it. Not as good as a teacher but definitely quite good for a three year-old whale. He knew he'd got quite good at making connections because he'd already made some connections on his own. He'd answered his own questions that had started with 'why,' without even having to ask a teacher.

One question he'd had was why he'd sometimes feel a little bit sad when playing with the other whales at playtime. To begin with, this was a confusing question because normally playing at playtime made whales feel happy. Not sad.

So he started trying to make connections to find the answer to his question. The first connection he made was that he felt a bit sad when the whales played racing at playtime. But most whales felt happy when they played racing. And Wellington was a whale, but he didn't feel happy, so he must need to make some more connections.

His first idea was that it might be something to do with the place. The whales always played their racing at the lagoon. The lagoon was a perfect place for racing because it had a kind of round, lagoony shape. This meant you could race laps if you wanted to. But it was also big enough that you could just race straight if you wanted to do that. Wellington liked these options.

Another nice thing about the lagoon was that sometimes other animals could sit on the bank and watch the whales playing racing. Wellington liked it when the other animals sat on the bank and watched.

So if he liked the most important features of the lagoon, Wellington understood that the place couldn't be the reason why he was feeling unhappy.

Then he realised that the children often seemed happy when they were racing extra fast. Swimmy, for example, was very good at racing extra fast and he often said how happy that made him. But Wellington never raced extra fast. He never even raced a bit fast. He always raced slowly and, if he tried to even race a bit fast, he just wobbled off the racing line and ended up racing even more slowly.

That was it. That was the moment he felt a bit sad. There was the connection. The really fast whales were happy, and the slow, wobbly whale was a bit sad.

Normally, Wellington would have been happy to have made this connection and to have worked out the answer to his question. Particularly because it was a question starting with 'why'. This time though, he couldn't help asking himself another question: Why did he wobble when he tried to swim extra fast, even though most whales swam extra fast when they tried to swim extra fast?

Wellington thought for a bit. And then – he wasn't sure why – but he suddenly remembered the way he'd been thinking when he'd spoken to his teacher about why the other children called him 'Wellington'. He'd been quite new at school then and hadn't learned to be good at making connections yet, so he'd needed his teacher to explain to him that the other children called him 'Wellington' because his tail looked a bit like a wellington boot.

Now he wasn't very new at school and now he had learned to be good at making connections. And now he realised that he didn't need his teacher to explain to him that he wobbled a bit when he tried to swim extra fast because his tail looked a bit like a wellington boot.

Wellington was a bit happy at having made the connections and at having answered his questions, but he was a bit sad about wobbling and a bit surprised at the reason for feeling sad being wobbling and the reason for wobbling being that his tail looked a bit like a wellington boot.

It was all very confusing. And as Wellington thought about how confusing it was, he realised that the wet on his face wasn't the normal wet from the normal water that whales are normally swimming around in anyway. There was a tear on his face. Wellington was crying.

OPPOSITES

Wellington liked opposites. He liked the way you could make them up. So, if something was funny or good or possible, you could make up the opposite, like 'unfunny' or 'ungood' or 'unpossible'. Very often the English teacher would say that we normally say 'bad' or 'impossible', but that didn't really bother Wellington. He was still happy at having made up the opposites and he just tried to remember to use the normal opposites the English teacher liked the next time the English teacher was listening.

Even more than making up the words for opposites, Wellington liked doing things with opposites. So if something was far away and he wanted to see it, he just had to make it unfar away, or near, if the English teacher was listening. And then he could see it. Or if he was eating something and not really enjoying it because it was a bit tasteless, he just needed to make it tasty, and then he could really enjoy it. 'Tasteless' and 'tasty' were very important opposites, so Wellington had learned quite quickly how to make something tasteless tasty – normally by dipping it in ketchup.

Wellington knew that the opposite of 'happy' was 'sad'. Or 'unhappy'. He didn't know why there were two opposites of 'happy', but the English teacher didn't seem to mind if you said 'sad' or if you said 'unhappy', even if she was listening quite closely.

That meant the opposite of 'sad' was 'happy'. 'Unsad' was another opposite the English teacher said wasn't normal, even though she didn't seem to mind 'unhappy'. Wellington didn't really understand why 'sad' only had one opposite, but 'happy' had two opposites. Maybe the opposite of 'one' was 'two'. He wasn't sure but it didn't really matter anyway.

What did matter – and what Wellington did really understand – was that if he could stop feeling sad, then he could start feeling the opposite, which was happy. He couldn't stop having a tail that looked a bit like a wellington boot, but he could stop trying to swim extra fast. He started stopping trying to swim extra fast by just watching the other whales racing, without racing himself.

But watching the other whales racing and swimming extra fast without wobbling didn't really stop him feeling sad. And it certainly didn't start him feeling happy. So Wellington decided to swim off and do something else. Wellington's dad had always said that swimming off and doing something else was a good thing to do if he ever felt angry or sad or cross or unhappy and he wanted to feel the opposite –- which was peaceful or happy or calm or happy.

So Wellington swam off on his own and looked for something else to do. As he'd swum off on his own, and as no-one was where he'd swum to, no-one was around, so he had plenty of space to do what he wanted to do, and he decided to see how far he could blow water out of his blowhole.

Wellington had always liked blowing water out of his blowhole, but he didn't really do it any more than most other whales. Wellington liked it though because, while some whales can blow two little squirts or one big burst or some other shape, Wellington had realised that he could do different kinds of squirts and bursts and other shapes. The only reason he didn't do it more often is that he didn't really have the time or the space. But now he did really have the time. And the space.

He started by blowing a long squirt of water as far as he could in front of him. Then he tilted a bit and blew some more water at a different angle. Then he blew some water straight up in the air. Then he did a little wobble while blowing and saw what happened when he did a double squirt at the same time.

Wellington carried on like this, squirting and spurting and splashing and sploshing – spraying out water in big bursts and giant jets and straight streams and scattergun salvos.

Wellington really enjoyed himself. His dad had been right. It had been a good thing to do to swim off and start doing something else. He'd stopped feeling sad. He'd started feeling happy.

PRACTICE

*P*ractice is a way of getting better at something. And getting better at something means you can do something better, which normally makes you happy. So practice should normally make you happy.

The problem with some practice is that the way to get better at something is to do something you're not very good at. And doing something you're not very good at can be very frustrating, which can make you sad or unhappy, and these are both opposites of happy, so not really what you want to be.

Wellington had experienced both kinds of practice. He liked to practise something he was already quite good at to get very good at it. But he didn't like to practise something he wasn't really any good at, just to try to get a little bit good at it. Wellington's dad had tried to make him practise the cello once, but Wellington hadn't really been any good at playing the cello and had kept getting frustrated and sad. So after a couple of weeks trying, his dad had stopped asking Wellington to practise the cello.

His dad understood, of course. He didn't really like doing things that he wasn't really any good at either. He'd just thought it would've been nice because Wellington's mum had loved playing the cello. But then she had been really quite good at it.

Wellington was really quite good at squirting water from his blowhole in a variety of interesting ways. And Wellington really enjoyed practising squirting water from his blowhole. And Wellington had a lot of time to practise. Most afternoons, the other whales would play racing and Wellington would swim off on his own to practise.

So Wellington got better and better. The PE teacher would often say that practice makes perfect. Wellington didn't really see how you could blow water out of your blowhole perfectly, but he definitely got better and better, and he definitely enjoyed it more and more.

Different angles and different shapes. Different heights and different lengths. Different sizes and different sounds. Different speeds and different strengths.

Wellington was truly happy practising. Only when he was finished – usually when he was tired and it was time to go home – did he notice how quiet it was when he stopped squirting water. Then Wellington would think about the quiet as he swam home, and he would quickly make the connection that it was quiet because there weren't any other whales there. And there weren't any other whales there because they were all having fun racing together, and he'd been the only whale who'd swum off to do something else.

He normally arrived home quite quickly though, which meant he normally arrived home before he had time to be sad or confused or lonely. And as his dad normally had tea ready by the time Wellington arrived home, and as his dad normally made krill and ketchup for tea, Wellington normally forgot about the quiet. Instead, he enjoyed the sound of a whale and his dad happily eating something which was the whale's favourite food. And which the dad also seemed to quite like, even if it wasn't anything very continental.

SHARING

When people talk about sharing, they mostly mean sharing something you've got with someone who hasn't got it. Sharing a cake means cutting it in two and each having some. Sharing a toy means letting someone else play with it as well.

There is a problem with sharing something you've got though. Quite a big problem. The problem is that sharing something you've got means that you don't have as much of it. You give someone some cake and have less cake yourself. Or you give someone your toy for a bit and you don't have the toy for a bit. And that can make you a bit unhappy.

The good thing about sharing something you've got is that it makes the person you share it with happy. Because they get some cake or they can play with a toy for a bit. And them being happy can make you happy too.

Another kind of sharing is better than sharing something you've got. This is sharing something you do.

When you share something you do, if it's a kind or fun or interesting something, then it can make the people you share it with happy or excited or at least interested. And them being happy or excited or at least interested can make you happy or excited, too. Or at least interested.

And when you share something you do, you still do just as much of it as when you don't share it. Other people watching or listening or joining in or helping doesn't normally stop you doing it at all. So there's no reason to be even a little bit unhappy, so you just stay happy. Or at least interested.

Wellington was really enjoying practising blowing water from his blowhole. It was fun and exciting. The only problem with it was he always did it on his own when the other whales were racing.

And the better he got, the more Wellington wanted to share his tricks with someone else. He thought his tricks were quite fun and exciting, or at least interesting. So he was sure sharing his tricks with someone else would make them happy and excited. Or at least interested.

Wellington was thinking exactly this one day when he'd just managed to perfect one of his tricks. The trick sent two droplet-shaped jets of water up and out at a slight angle so that they overlapped in a heart shape. He was thinking he'd perfected it when he remembered he wasn't sure if you could do things like this perfectly, but he'd certainly done it very well indeed.

He was just thinking how very well indeed he'd done it, when a voice interrupted his thinking.

"Wow! What was that?"

The voice belonged to one of the other whales from school, Reef.

Wellington looked around and was just going to ask Reef why he wasn't racing with the other whales when he saw a bandage around Reef's left flipper and quickly made the connection that whales with bandages around their flippers probably didn't normally race very much.

"That was one of my tricks. It's called 'hydro heart'," Wellington said, finally getting around to answering Reef's question.

"It was amazing!" said Reef. "Where did you learn to do that, Wellington?"

"I learned to do it here. I practise here most days when you and the other whales are racing at the lagoon. I can do lots of other tricks, too."

Then Wellington shared a few other tricks with Reef. He didn't share lots of his other tricks straight away because first he wanted to check whether sharing his tricks was going to do what he thought. But it did. Reef got very happy and excited, which did make Wellington even happier and even more excited.

After Wellington had shared a few tricks, Reef asked him if he could come back the next day and watch again. Wellington said of course he could, but that he shouldn't come until about 2.30, because Wellington liked to wait an hour or so after eating before blowing water out of his blowhole. Reef said he understood because his dad had often told him he wasn't supposed to do anything complicated after eating, and Wellington's tricks hadn't just looked amazing, but very complicated, too. And then he swam off.

The next day, at about 2.30, Reef came back and watched again. And he brought a few other whales with him. And Wellington saw that the few other whales didn't have bandages around their left flippers.

"We've all come to see your show, Wellington!" Reef said. The other whales all looked very excited so Reef must have told them all about Wellington's tricks.

"Reef's told us all about your tricks, Wellington!" said one of the other whales. And then they were quiet and seemed to be waiting for the show to begin.

Wellington was so excited that he even felt a little nervous, but mainly he felt extremely happy to be able to share his tricks with some other whales. And he was extremely happy that his tricks were now a show because now he had someone to show them to. And the other whales were extremely happy to be able to see Wellington's really quite wonderful tricks.

The next day, the few other whales became a few more other whales. And the day after that, the few more other whales became really quite a lot of other whales.

Soon, Wellington was giving his show every day at about 2.30, with a nice, settled stomach, to lots of other whales. Not always the same other whales. But always lots. And sharing his different ways of blowing water out of his blowhole made Wellington really happy. So he kept practising and kept getting better and better, and kept inventing more and more new tricks.

Wellington's show became so important for him that he spent most mornings looking forward to about 2.30. And he spent most afternoons enjoying what had happened that day at about 2.30. And he didn't spend any time at all any more thinking about how he wobbled a bit whenever he tried to swim extra fast because his tail looked a bit like a wellington boot. Wellington was happy.

COMPETITIONS

Wellington liked competitions. He liked it when he had the chance to do something he thought he was doing really well and then see if other people thought it was really good, too.

Luckily for Wellington, the teachers at school liked competitions, too. They didn't really do any of the doing things really well, but what they did do a lot of was saying whether they thought things were good. They enjoyed that, it seemed.

There wasn't a competition at school every week, but this week there was – it was the PE teacher's idea. He announced it in assembly, which was where all the whales at the school got together. Since all the whales at the school,

when they all got together, were very big, and
too big to fit in any of the classrooms, they got
together outside the school, where there was
plenty of space for everyone. There was even
space for a stage at the front.

"We are going to have a competition!" the
PE teacher announced. Wellington was very
excited. Then the PE teacher said, "We are
going to have a special day for the whole school
with lots of racing and jumping. It will be a
whole day of competitions!"

Wellington was a little bit disappointed.
He liked competitions, but racing and jumping
were two of the things that he – even when he
tried to do them really well – usually ended up
not doing very well at all. And the teachers and
everyone else would also think that he hadn't
done them very well at all. And they'd clap and
cheer for the other whales who had raced or
jumped better. So they'd clap and cheer for the
other whales who didn't have wobbly tails that
looked a bit like wellington boots.

Wellington was concentrating so hard on being a little disappointed that he almost didn't hear the PE teacher say,

"But before the whole day of competitions, we need another competition! A naming competition!"

Hearing this – because Wellington did just about hear it – Wellington stopped being a little disappointed and started being really quite excited. A naming competition sounded like something he might be really good at.

All the children were invited to take part in the naming competition – to name the day of competitions. The PE teacher called it the 'day of competitions naming competition', which made Wellington think maybe it would've been a good idea to have a competition to name the naming competition, but probably that would've been a bit too complicated.

The children had one week to think up their entries, with each child allowed to enter one name in the competition. The PE teacher and the English teacher would then select the winner. The PE teacher would be looking for a name that described the day of competitions well and the English teacher would be looking for what she called 'linguistic elegance'. That meant it should sound good, but they couldn't say 'sound good' because that wouldn't have been linguistically elegant enough for the English teacher.

The children were very excited. Some were excited about the day of competitions and some were excited about the naming competition. There were some who weren't all that excited because they didn't like competitions, but they just wouldn't take part. So they weren't excited, but they didn't really mind too much.

Wellington was particularly excited. He had a whole week to think about his entry. His first idea was 'School Runnings', which he had thought was quite funny because he'd once seen a film called 'Cool Runnings'. And 'school' was a good word to have in the name because it was being organised at school. But then he had thought that the PE teacher probably wouldn't like it because not all the competitions involved running. In fact, as the competitors were all likely to be whales, there was not likely be much running at all. Except for the kind of fast swimming that whales sometimes called 'running'. But it wasn't really running, so maybe 'School Runnings' didn't really describe the day of competitions very well.

After 'School Runnings', Wellington had lots of other ideas, but he didn't tell anyone any of them, because he wanted to make sure it was completely his idea, and not have someone say something to change it. And because he had a whole week, he spent some of it thinking about other things, too. A week is a long time just to spend thinking up competition names. Well, a long time for a young whale anyway.

GOALS

Reaching goals means doing something you wanted to do. Normally, it even means managing to do something you wanted to do which wasn't very easy.

The idea – what is supposed to happen when you reach a goal – is that it makes you happy. Normally you wanted to be happy, which is why you wanted to do the thing you wanted to do, because you thought it would make you happy. And it normally does make you happy. At least to begin with.

Also, if you do reach a goal that you've had, then you usually get an extra bit of happiness just for having reached it, which is nice.

That's how it was with Wellington. He had wanted people to call him 'Wellington', and he'd managed to make people call him 'Wellington'. So now he was happy in general that he'd managed to make people call him 'Wellington', and he was happy specifically every time someone called him 'Wellington' — which was quite often.

As with lots of things that happen quite often, however, it wasn't long before it became so normal that it stopped making Wellington happy every single time someone called him 'Wellington'. It didn't make him unhappy. He just stopped really noticing it.

Oddly enough, after a while, it actually started making him happy when someone accidentally called him 'Oslo', because it gave him a chance to say 'Wellington', and it reminded him that he'd managed to get everyone to call him 'Wellington'. And having managed to get everyone to call him 'Wellington' had made him really quite happy.

WINNING

A week must have passed since the competitions had been announced because the whales were outside the school in assembly again and it was time for them to make their entries in the naming competition and find out who would win. Wellington liked winning – mainly because it meant that other people thought he'd done something really well. He was really very excited.

By now, most of the children had started calling the naming competition 'the name comp', which wasn't very elegant – linguistically speaking – but then there were no prizes to be won. The children just didn't want to have to say 'day of competitions naming competition' every time they talked about it.

The PE teacher and the English teacher had made a plan for the assembly. All the children who had prepared an entry were going to line up in alphabetical order and take turns going onto the stage to tell everyone what their entry was. Then, if the PE teacher thought it described the day of competitions well and the English teacher thought it was linguistically elegant enough, then that child would wait on the stage amongst the finalists. Once all the finalists were there, the other teachers and the other children would join in and talk about which entry they liked best. Then, after listening to everyone, the PE teacher and the English teacher would decide on the winner. This was how most important decisions were taken at the school, so everyone would be familiar with the process and no-one would question the fairness or legitimacy of the outcome.

Wellington, being called 'Wellington', was up second-last with his entry. Only one whale entering the competition came after him alphabetically. This whale was called 'Yngling'.

Some of the teachers hadn't been too happy about putting Wellington under W when doing the alphabetical order. Some said he should still be under O, because Oslo was his name really – 'officially', they called it. But after Wellington had made it quite clear to everyone – even the headteacher – that his name was definitely 'Wellington', the teachers all agreed together to let Wellington go under W for alphabetical ordering purposes. Which kept Wellington happy and actually turned out much less confusing for everyone.

The most interesting of the first few entries in the name comp was 'Day of competitions with lots of racing and jumping'. The PE teacher got very excited about this entry because he said it described the day perfectly. Unfortunately for Dogger, the whale whose entry it was, the English teacher said it wasn't linguistically elegant enough, so Dogger didn't get to wait on the stage and didn't get to be one of the finalists.

By the time Wellington's turn came along, there were already two finalists on stage. Their two entries were 'Sports Day' and 'Whales Got Talent'. Wellington quite liked 'Whales Got Talent', but he thought his entry was good too, so he was happy to go on stage and announce,

"The Whalympics!"

There was a short pause. Then the PE teacher and the English teacher both nodded at each other and Wellington stayed on the stage with the other finalists.

The last remaining entrant was Yngling. He felt just as happy as Wellington had just felt when he went onto the stage and said confidently,

"The 1st Yngling Cup!"

Yngling always liked to use the word 'Yngling' as often as possible. He liked his name and he didn't think people said it enough, so he was hoping that having his name in the name of the day of competitions would make people say it far more often than usual.

Unfortunately for Yngling, the PE teacher shook his head in disapproval and, even though the English teacher thought it sounded good and said she quite liked it from a linguistic point of view, the PE teacher waved Yngling off the stage.

Fortunately for Yngling, as often happened, a group of children sitting somewhere near the back of the assembly starting chanting 'Yngling, Yngling, Yngling, Yngling' as he left the stage. This meant that people had ended up saying 'Yngling' lots after all, and Yngling turned out perfectly happy with the outcome of the name comp.

The discussion of the three finalists' entries started with everyone chattering amongst themselves in a fairly disorderly fashion. This was how most discussions began because it was a good way of letting everyone talk about their initial reactions with the people near them, as well as creating enough general noise for people who wanted to talk about other things to talk about the other things they wanted to talk about.

Once the discussion moved on to a more coherent stage, it turned out that 'Sports Day' was very popular, until someone asked if there was an apostrophe in there anywhere. Everyone looked at the English teacher, who said,

"Well, of course. Of course. Clearly there should be an apostrophe before the final 's' because we have a 'day of sport' so it's a genitive singular. Sport. Apostrophe. S. Day."

Unfortunately for the English teacher, someone then asked whether that was right though because there might be more than one sport. And then someone else asked whether it wouldn't actually be more linguistically elegant to just not have an apostrophe at all. And then someone else asked, if you weren't using an apostrophe at all, then why not call it 'Sport Day' without an 's' at all.

The English teacher listened to all of this and thought that it must be very confusing because she was an English teacher and even she was finding it quite confusing. So, after listening and thinking for a bit, she said,

"'Sports Day' is too generic and not linguistically elegant enough. The other entries are both much better."

And because she didn't say anything about it being confusing, but managed to say it in a very authoritative way like an English teacher who knew exactly what they were talking about, everyone agreed with her.

The whale whose idea it had been just said 'OK' and swam off the stage.

The English teacher naturally felt pleased about how she'd handled this problem, even though she felt a bit sorry for the whale who had suggested 'Sports Day'. And she still felt a bit confused about whether there should be an apostrophe in there anywhere or not.

Wellington naturally felt a bit pleased about being one of the last two remaining

finalists, even though he also felt a bit sorry
for the whale who had suggested 'Sports Day'.
He'd quite liked that suggestion. He definitely
preferred the name 'Whalympics' though, and
was hopeful that other people would prefer
it too and it would be chosen as the winning
entry.

Being a bit pleased and a bit sorry at the
same time made the situation a bit confusing –
not confusing enough to make him cry though.

Judging from the initial excitement,
'Whales Got Talent' was a very popular
name as well. Lots of whales liked the way it
sounded like a popular TV show, but included
the word 'whales'. Then someone mentioned
that the word 'Whalympics' also included most
of the word 'whales', so you couldn't really
prefer 'Whales Got Talent' just because it
mentioned whales.

Then someone asked if there was an
apostrophe anywhere in 'Whales Got Talent'.

Everyone looked at the English teacher
again, who, luckily for her, had been thinking

about the possibility of apostrophes in the last
two entries ever since getting a bit confused
over 'Sports Day'.

The English teacher said,

"In 'Britain's Got Talent', the 'apostrophe s'
replaces the word 'has'. In 'Whale's Got Talent',
'apostrophe s' would therefore mean that just
one whale has talent. Which isn't what we
want the name of our day of competitions to
say. We are having lots of competitions so lots
of whales will have talent so 'whales' should be
plural. That means it should be 'Whales've Got
Talent", with 'apostrophe V E'. 'Whales Got
Talent' without any apostrophe might sound
OK the first time you hear it but it isn't really
good enough grammar for me – as an English
teacher – to possibly be able to let it be the
winning entry."

This meant that Wellington's entry was
the only entry left which could win. So it won.
Someone said that an Olympiad was only
every four years, which wasn't very good if
they wanted to have their day of competitions

every year. But then another someone pointed out – quite correctly – that a Whalympiad could easily be every year or every term or however often they wanted to have their day of competitions.

The PE teacher was happy because they'd found a name for the day of competitions which nicely described the day of competitions.

The English teacher was happy because she'd finally stopped being confused and managed to give such a good answer about apostrophes, which had made her look like a really good English teacher who knew exactly what she was talking about.

The headteacher was happy too, even though the assembly had dragged on for too long and eaten into valuable lesson time. She was mainly happy because she seemed to have a really good English teacher at her school who seemed to know exactly what she was talking about.

Wellington, though, was the happiest of all – particularly since the bell rang as they were leaving assembly, which meant that it was time for lunch. Which meant that it was time for krill and ketchup. Which meant that all the other whales were happy, too.

EXPECTING

Winning the name comp had made him happy, but the happiest Wellington had been was when the whales had started coming to see his water squirting show at about 2.30. He'd been happy not just because he'd been able to share what he'd been doing, but also because it had been so unexpected.

He had sometimes thought that it would be nice to be able to share what he'd been doing, but he hadn't even started thinking about how it could happen. And as he hadn't even started thinking about how it could happen, he certainly hadn't started thinking that it might happen. Which is why it had been so very unexpected.

The opposite of unexpected is expected.
After lots of whales had started coming every
day at about 2.30 to see Wellington's show, he
had started expecting them to come. And they
did come, too. It was expected. Which meant
it still made Wellington happy and excited,
but without the extra dash of happiness and
excitement that he'd had when it had still been
unexpected.

Reef felt the same way. He still loved
coming to Wellington's show, but he
expected to love coming to it now. He didn't
normally feel the extra dash of happiness
and excitement that he'd felt the first time
when – completely unexpectedly – he'd seen
Wellington do his special trick, hydro heart,
for the first time. The show was still good,
particularly when Wellington did hydro heart,
but now it was expected.

One particularly good thing about
something being unexpected is that, if it
doesn't happen, then you almost don't even
realise that it hasn't happened. Because you

weren't expecting it to happen anyway. So it doesn't happen, but you don't get sad or disappointed or even cross. You normally just stay in whatever mood you were in anyway.

As expected is the opposite of unexpected, there is one particularly bad thing about something being expected. If it doesn't happen, then you do realise quite strongly that it hasn't happened, because you were expecting it to happen. So it doesn't happen, and you do get sad or disappointed or even cross. You normally forget whatever mood you were in before and end up quite unhappy.

This is just what happened to Wellington one day when, at about 2.30, he was ready to do his show, but no other whales were there for him to share it with. He was so sad and disappointed about not having anyone to share his water squirting with that he didn't even do any water squirting. Instead, he did some thinking.

Wellington didn't need to think about why he was sad and disappointed. He knew

straight away that it was because he'd been
expecting to share his water squirting show
with other whales and that there weren't any
other whales to share his water squirting
show with. Wellington wanted to think about
why there weren't any other whales.

Wellington started by thinking that if the
other whales weren't there where he was, then
they must be somewhere else where he wasn't.
And as they weren't watching his show, then
they must be doing something else as well.

Most days, the whales who didn't come to
Wellington's show at about 2.30 were racing
and practising their fast swimming at the
lagoon. So Wellington thought if today was
like most days, then that's what the whales
who weren't at his show would be doing.

The only difference between today and
most days was that all the whales – except
for Wellington – weren't at his show. So all
the whales – except for Wellington – must be
racing and practising their fast swimming at
the lagoon.

Thinking this helped Wellington to make the connections that answered his question why no whales were at his show. They were all racing and practising their fast swimming at the lagoon because they were all getting ready for the Whalympics – the big day of competitions. And Wellington wasn't getting ready for the Whalympics because Wellington wasn't going to be taking part in the big day of competitions. And Wellington wasn't going to be taking part in the big day of competitions because Wellington wobbled when he tried to swim extra fast. And Wellington wobbled when he tried to swim extra fast because Wellington's tail looked a bit like a wellington boot.

Wellington was pleased to have made these connections but he was a bit sad about the reason why no one was there. He thought it would be a good idea to have a competition for squirting water but then he remembered that everyone was so busy getting ready for the Whalympics that they probably didn't have time for another competition just at the moment. Everyone except Wellington.

While Wellington had been thinking all this, and while he had been making all these connections, he hadn't realised that he'd swum home. But when he did realise that he'd swum home, he was pleased that he'd swum home, because his dad had prepared some krill and ketchup for tea. And Wellington liked krill and ketchup.

FAIRNESS

I t's not always easy to be fair. Being fair can sometimes be very complicated. In fact, being fair is often what makes it so difficult to be someone who people expect to be fair. Someone like a mum or a dad or a teacher.

Mums and dads and teachers are supposed to try to be as fair as possible to children. Sometimes this is fairly easy. If one child gets an ice cream, then it's normally fair for the other children to get an ice cream, too. If they want one. And if they like ice cream.

Even being fair with ice cream can be a bit complicated though. If one child doesn't like ice cream or says they don't want an ice cream, then the mum or the dad or the teacher has to decide whether it would be fair to get them something else instead. Which isn't always easy. Particularly if they're at an ice cream shop that only really sells ice cream.

Or sometimes every child gets an ice cream but then one child drops their ice cream after having had only two licks. Then the mum or the dad or the teacher has to decide whether it would be fair to get that child a second ice cream. Or whether it would be fair to say, "Sorry, but every child only gets one ice cream."

It's not easy being fair.

The teachers at Wellington's school usually tried to be fair to all the children. The headteacher always told them that trying to be fair to all the children was very important and they usually tried to do what the headteacher told them was very important.

About a month before the Whalympics were set to take place, the three teachers who were in charge of organising the Whalympics had a talk about how to make sure the Whalympics were as fair as possible.

The three teachers who were in charge of organising the Whalympics were the PE teacher, the English teacher and the art teacher. It had been the PE teacher's idea, so he was involved. The English teacher had helped with the name comp and had had a few other good ideas, so she was involved. And then they'd asked the art teacher to help, because he was very good at organising things.

The PE teacher thought it was a bit unusual for an art teacher to be very good at organising things, but the English teacher had said that it didn't matter how unusual it was. What mattered was how good at organising things the art teacher was. And he was very good.

As happened quite a lot, all three teachers knew there was a problem – making sure the Whalympics were as fair as possible – but they didn't all know how to solve this problem. So, as also happened quite a lot, they had a meeting to talk about it.

They started off their meeting with a few simple rules for fairness. The English teacher wrote everything down so they wouldn't forget anything and so that if anyone asked what they were doing to make sure the Whalympics were as fair as possible, they could tell them.

The first simple rule was:

'Any whale who wants to take part in the Whalympics can take part in the Whalympics.'

That sounded quite fair. Though it did mean – or at least suggest – that other animals who wanted to take part in the Whalympics probably couldn't take part in the Whalympics.

Was that fair?

After thinking for a bit, they agreed that it probably was fair because they were all whales and all the children at the school were all whales and that was who the Whalympics were being organised for. To make it clear, they changed the rule a little bit to:

'All whale children from our school who want to take part in the Whalympics can take part in the Whalympics.'

The English teacher liked starting with the word 'all' as well, because 'all' was a very fair-sounding word.

Another good thing about saying 'all whale children' was that it included boys and girls equally. And being fair to boys and girls equally was particularly important. When they were thinking about being fair to boys and girls equally, the English teacher asked whether the boys should race and jump against the girls or whether there should be separate races and jumping competitions for boys and separate races and jumping competitions for girls.

The art teacher said he wasn't sure which was fairer. If everyone raced and jumped together, it might be easier to organise, but he was sure that they would manage if there were different races and jumping competitions for boys and different races and jumping competitions for girls. He was very good at organising things.

The PE teacher said that girl whales and boy whales often had differently sized and shaped fins, flippers and flukes. And he said this could often affect how fast they raced and how high they jumped. This didn't mean all boys were slower than all girls or anything like that, but there were differences. It had been like that ever since he'd started teaching PE, which had been quite a long time ago. The English teacher thought this would be a good chance to say something clever about 'sexual dimorphism' but then she decided not to because she didn't really know enough about it.

This meant that if the boys and girls raced and jumped together, then whales with more suitable fins, flippers and flukes would be racing and jumping against whales with less suitable fins, flippers and flukes. Which didn't seem quite fair. But if they had separate races and jumping competitions for boys and girls, then all the whales with suitable fins, flippers and flukes would be together, and all the whales with less suitable fins, flippers and

flukes would be together. And it would mean
that half the races and jumping competitions
would be won by boys and half would be won by
girls. They agreed that that seemed fairer. They
weren't quite sure, but the English teacher
wrote it down anyway. The headteacher always
said that it was important to try to be as fair
as possible. And they were definitely trying.
It was hard to know whether there might be
a different way of doing it that might actually
be even fairer. But they were definitely trying.
That was the important thing.

Another question of fairness was who
should get a prize. One idea was that everyone
who competed should get a prize because if
everyone gets the same, then that's normally
fair. But the PE teacher said that it wasn't
really fair on the winners if they didn't get a
special prize for winning.

In the end, they agreed that it would be fair
if everyone got something according to where
they finished in their competition. So the first
three in each race or jumping competition

would get a prize for finishing in the first three, but all the other whales who competed would also get something for competing. That sounded fair.

Once that was decided, it also seemed fair if the whales who didn't compete didn't get anything for not competing. They had already said that all whale children who wanted to take part could take part. So it meant all whale children who didn't want to take part didn't have to take part. But then the English teacher asked,

"What about Wellington?"

"Wellington?" asked the PE teacher.

"Yes, Wellington," said the English teacher.

The three teachers all knew without having to say it to each other that Wellington wouldn't want to take part in the Whalympics because they all knew without having to say it to each other that Wellington felt sad when he tried to swim fast. And they also all knew that this was because he wobbled a bit because his tail looked a bit like a wellington boot.

The PE teacher began by saying that their first rule said that whales who wanted to take part could take part. So if Wellington didn't want to take part, he didn't have to take part. Just like any other whale who didn't want to.

But Wellington wasn't just like any other whale who didn't want to. No other whales who didn't want to had a tail that looked a bit like a wellington boot.

The art teacher remembered that the name 'Whalympics' had been Wellington's entry in the name comp. So he thought Wellington would probably be happy every time someone said the name 'Whalympics'. A bit like how Yngling was always happy whenever anyone said the name 'Yngling'. And during the Whalympics people were probably going to be saying the name 'Whalympics' very often, which would make Wellington happy very often.

It wouldn't make Yngling very happy but the teachers were worrying about Wellington at the moment.

The English teacher agreed with the art teacher but she still wasn't sure whether that made everything fair. Whoever had won the name comp would've felt happy when the winning entry was said on the day of competitions. That had been the prize for the winner of the name comp and didn't really have anything to do with Wellington and the fact that his tail looked a bit like a wellington boot.

Now all the teachers had said something and so now no-one said anything for a little bit. They sat there, thinking about how complicated it could be trying to be fair.

Then they started thinking about other things, but still didn't say anything.

Then the art teacher did say something:

"I do like the name, 'Whalympics'."

The other teachers still didn't say anything so the art teacher kept talking.

"I like the way it sounds like 'Olympics'. We should do things with that. The prizes could be gold, silver and bronze medals. We could have Whalympic Rings and have an opening ceremony and light a Whalympic Torch, we could ..."

Then, even though the art teacher still seemed to be talking, the English teacher did say something. She asked,

"At the opening ceremony? Are we having an opening ceremony?"

"Well, I'm sure I could organise one," replied the art teacher.

The PE teacher and the English teacher were sure the art teacher could organise one, too. He was very good at organising things.

"Well, that's it!" cried the English teacher.

"That's how we can be fair to Wellington! He can be the star of the opening ceremony!"

This was such a good idea that the three teachers didn't have to talk about it for very long. They all knew that Wellington could do very exciting tricks by squirting and blowing water. And that he liked sharing these tricks. And that the other whales liked watching. So this idea would make everyone happy and excited. So the English teacher wrote it down straight away. And she liked writing things down, so that made her happy.

When, the next day, the PE teacher asked Wellington if he would like to be the star of the Whalympic opening ceremony, he agreed straight away that it was a good idea, said 'thank you', and swam right off to practise some special Whalympic squirting. Wellington was happy again.

When the headteacher asked the PE teacher what they were doing to try to make the Whalympics fair, the PE teacher showed her everything the English teacher had written down. Everything about the rules, about the races and jumping competitions for boys and the races and jumping competitions for girls, and about Wellington. The headteacher said these were good rules, said 'thank you' and then swam off to do something else. The headteacher usually had something else to do, and she didn't have to talk much about the rules, because she was happy with them. And not having to talk much about the rules made the PE teacher happy too.

That morning, the art teacher was also thinking about the Whalympics, and he was thinking that there was still a lot of organising to do. He also thought that so far they had had lots of good ideas and had been organising things very well. He was a bit hungry though, so first he swam off to get some lunch. And the art teacher liked lunch, so he was happy too.

SURPRISE

Wellington spent the weeks before the Whalympics practising what he was going to do in the opening ceremony. He wanted it to be exciting and surprising for everyone who was going to be there. Fortunately, the other whales were mostly practising racing and jumping at the lagoon, so Wellington didn't have anyone watching and seeing anything which might've made the actual ceremony any less exciting or any less surprising.

Unfortunately, Wellington wasn't really sure exactly what to do. He knew that he had some tricks that most of the whales really liked and which, if he didn't do, they would be disappointed. He also knew, however,

that if he did too may tricks that most of the
whales already knew, even if they liked them,
then they would be disappointed because the
ceremony wouldn't be surprising enough.

All the PE teacher had told Wellington was
that he had ten minutes for his part of the
ceremony, and he could do whatever he liked.
So long as it was exciting and surprising.
And at the end he had to light the Whalympic
Torch.

Wellington had never lit a Whalympic
Torch before so he'd had to ask the art teacher,
who was actually organising the opening
ceremony, what a Whalympic Torch was
exactly and how you lit it exactly. Then he had
to work out how to light it in an exciting and
surprising way. The good thing about never
having lit a Whalympic Torch before was
nobody had ever seen him light a Whalympic
Torch before either. So that bit of the ceremony
should definitely be surprising for everyone.
For everyone except Wellington. Wellington
had to do lots of planning and practising

to make sure that, for him, the ceremony wouldn't be surprising at all.

The Whalympics were being held at the lagoon. Not only was the lagoon the best place for swimming fast, the lagoon was also the best place for the audience. This is because much of the audience wasn't made up of whales, but of other animals. And other animals, many other animals anyway, don't like sitting in the water but prefer to sit on a piece of land when they are watching a major sporting event.

The only problem with the lagoon was that some whales like to swim up from quite a deep depth before jumping. And the lagoon was quite shallow so all the whales would have to swim up from quite a shallow depth before jumping. The PE teacher said this was how most whales normally did it anyway – and this was the proper way to jump he taught in his PE lessons, where he called it 'breaching'. Because in a PE lesson you are supposed to use proper words for proper things. This meant it would add something good and educational to the Whalympics if the whales all had to jump in the proper way. Particularly if they called it 'breaching'.

The art teacher said the lagoon was good too, because setting up temporary structures was easier in shallower water. He was very good at organising things but he still didn't want the things he was organising to be unnecessarily complicated, so he arranged for a nice temporary structure with a bar to be set up in the lagoon where the water was quite shallow, but still deep enough for whales to breach in the proper way. While he was doing this arranging, he also arranged for some banners and flagpoles and other lighting and sound equipment to be installed around the lagoon, so that everyone would remember they were at the Whalympics and be able to see and hear what was going on.

With the temporary structure and other equipment added, the lagoon was almost perfect. It had a big round area of water for the racing competitions, it had somewhere for the breaching competitions, and it had land around it where the audience could sit to watch. There was, thanks to a good idea the art teacher had had, also a bit of water for whales and other animals that did like sitting in the water, like fish, to sit in. So they could watch the Whalympics as well.

The art teacher, English teacher and PE teacher had all agreed that it was important to have as big an audience as possible, so that not only the whales taking part in the competitions would enjoy the Whalympics. This was one of the points they had come up with when they were thinking about how to make the Whalympics as fair as possible, and one which had made the headteacher particularly happy. So they were particularly happy that the lagoon had been available to hold the Whalympics.

Wellington had been told about the lagoon being the place where the Whalympics were being held as soon as it had been decided on.

This meant that Wellington had plenty of time
to prepare his opening ceremony especially
for the lagoon. This meant that, when it was
time for him to perform his opening ceremony,
it was perfectly matched to the place where
it was happening. Which not only made
Wellington happy, but also the whole audience,
because Wellington had made sure that his
performance made them happy, too.

And it really did.

Wellington's show managed to include
enough of the other whales' favourite tricks
to meet their expectations and make them
happy. They saw what they wanted to see. And
it also included a few other tricks or tricks
in slightly unusual orders, which surprised
the whales enough to keep them excited.
The other animals who had come to watch
the Whalympics didn't really know about
Wellington's shows or how he could squirt
water in such spectacular ways, so they were
very surprised and very impressed and very
excited for the whole ceremony.

One highlight of Wellington's opening ceremony, which was also the final trick, was one that none of the other whales or other animals had seen before. Wellington hadn't even ever done it before. He'd practised it a few times but not really done it for real. The reason he hadn't really done it for real was because it was the trick of lighting the Whalympic Torch.

The Whalympic Torch had been the art teacher's idea, when he'd said that it would be nice to have a few things in the Whalympics that were like things they have in the Olympics. They had the Whalympic Rings, which were five rings that looked a bit like the Olympic Rings, they had gold, silver and bronze medals, and they had the Whalympic Torch, which was a flame which was supposed to burn throughout the Whalympics.

But before it can burn throughout the Whalympics, it first has to be lit during the opening ceremony. And as Wellington was going to be performing the opening ceremony,

Wellington had to light the Whalympic Torch.

As lighting the Whalympic Torch came at the end of the ceremony, all the other tricks came before it. The trick just before it was Wellington creating the Whalympic Rings with water. He couldn't do five bursts at the same time, but he did work out how to do five circular bursts in a row very quickly so that they overlapped in the air and looked like the five rings linked together. So that's how Wellington made the Whalympic Rings and it was a great success.

After the five very quick bursts to make the Whalympic Rings, Wellington's trick to light the Whalympic Torch was much less explosive, but with a very exciting ending. His idea had been to spray water strongly, but very carefully and precisely, at a special triangular mirror hanging above the lagoon. The jet of water would turn the mirror slowly so that it would catch the sun. The mirror would be lined up with the torch so that when Wellington had turned it just right, a strong beam of sunlight would concentrate onto the top of the Whalympic Torch and it would be set alight. That was his idea and it had been a bit complicated, but he had got help from the physics teacher, who was good at complicated things, and from the art teacher, who had arranged for everything to be set up properly. So that's how Wellington lit the Whalympic Torch and it was a great success, too.

Everyone was certainly very excited and impressed by the opening ceremony because afterwards they all talked about how excited and impressed they had been. And Wellington had been very excited as well, and very nicely surprised that it had all gone so well, even though he had only practised it in practice before.

The English teacher and the art teacher, who were sitting next to each other during the opening ceremony, talked to each other a bit about how poetic it was. They thought that using a stream of water to light a fire was a wonderful symbol, as fire and water are traditionally opposite elements. Wellington knew a lot about opposites but he hadn't really thought about poetry when he had been thinking of ideas of how to light the Whalympic Torch. Wellington had just thought that, as his whole show was squirting water in different ways, it made sense to do something particularly special like lighting the Whalympic Torch by squirting water in a particularly special way. He didn't mind people thinking it was poetic though. He didn't mind poetry.

Someone else who didn't mind poetry was the maths teacher, but she hadn't been thinking about it. She'd been thinking about geometry instead. She thought it was very nice having different shapes in the ceremony like circular rings and a triangular mirror. She decided not to say anything to anyone about it because she was sitting next to the PE teacher, and he was concentrating on organising the competitions so he probably didn't want to be distracted. And geometry can be very distracting.

After the opening ceremony, Wellington was very happy because all the parts of his show that were supposed to be surprising had been as surprising as they were supposed to be. And all the parts of his show that were supposed to be expected had been as expected as they were supposed to be. He wasn't sure if it had gone perfectly but it had gone very well indeed. And, at the end of the opening ceremony, when the whole audience was clapping and cheering, he felt particularly happy, not just because he realised that the audience's clapping and cheering meant he'd made them all happy, but because he felt like the real star of the Whalympics.

This happiness only lasted for a moment. Straight after the end of the opening ceremony, the PE teacher announced the start of the first actual competition. And straight after the PE teacher announced the start of the first actual competition, Wellington remembered that he wasn't actually taking part in any of the actual competitions. Wellington wasn't sad straight away but he did realise quite quickly that he probably wasn't actually going to be the real star of the Whalympics at all. So even though he wasn't sad, he did stop being happy.

SELFISHNESS

Everyone can be selfish sometimes. Most children are told by their parents and sometimes by other grown-ups not to be selfish. One way of not being selfish is to share, which isn't always easy, particularly if it means you end up with less of whatever it is you're sharing. But if you do manage to share, then it is nice because at least it stops you being selfish.

One part of being selfish is trying to make sure that you – yourself – are happy. The trick to not being selfish is to make sure that you – yourself – are happy, without making other people unhappy. Because if you're happy but someone else is unhappy, then on the whole, people aren't really any happier than if no one was happy in the first place.

So that's why it's no good being selfish.

Another kind of being selfish is when you get sad or cross when you see other people being happy. And this isn't because they're being mean or because they're trying to make you unhappy – you just feel a bit sad or cross because they're feeling so happy.

Wellington was thinking about this and about whether being sad and cross meant he was being selfish. He had been watching the competitions. He'd watched a couple of swimming competitions, one where they'd swum forwards and one where they'd swum backwards, and they had both been quite exciting.

Swimmy had won the one where they'd swum forwards because he'd swum faster than all the others. Swimmy seemed to be a very fast swimmer and Swimmy had been given a gold medal.

In fact, Wellington hadn't been watching but he later found out that Swimmy had won two races and been given two gold medals. One for swimming forwards a short way and one for swimming forwards a slightly longer way.

The PE teacher and the English teacher had had to decide how many swimming forwards races to have and how far they should all be. That had been one of the hardest things to decide when trying to make the Whalympics fair. In the end, they decided that there was nothing unfair about having a few different swimming forwards races because some whales might be better at swimming forwards further than others. And if the same whale did win more than one, then there would be nothing unfair about that whale getting more than one medal, which was what happened with Swimmy.

Wellington hadn't seen Swimmy's second race because he'd swum off to be a bit cross and angry and think about whether that meant he was being selfish. He didn't really think he was being selfish, but he was still cross and angry. And not very happy at all.

And not being happy made him even more unhappy because he had very much wanted to be happy during the Whalympics.

He did realise that most of the other whales were very happy and very much enjoying the Whalympics. Even the whales who hadn't won the races he'd watched seemed fairly happy. Particularly the ones who had got silver and bronze medals. But this still didn't make Wellington feel happy, for some reason. Maybe he really was being selfish.

Wellington had been right. Most of the other whales had been enjoying the Whalympics. The whales that were taking part in the competitions had been. And the whales – and the other animals – who had been watching had been. Even the PE teacher, the English teacher and the art teacher, who had been putting a lot of effort into the organisation, had been enjoying themselves and feeling very happy that everything seemed to be going so well. And the fact that everything seemed to be going so well made the headteacher very happy as well. She liked it when things went well.

Unfortunately, just as everyone was feeling very happy, there was an accident. It happened during one of the jumping competitions, where two whales had to jump up over the bar of the temporary structure, spin round together and land in the water together. They called the competition 'synchronised breaching'. And while trying to breach in a synchronised way, one of the whales had breached in the opposite way, in an asynchronous way, as the English teacher explained afterwards, and this asynchronous breaching had made the whale bump into the temporary structure and knock it over.

Just knocking over the temporary structure would have been quite unfortunate, but then the temporary structure fell into a pole with a flag with the Whalympic Rings on it, which was very unfortunate. And then the flagpole fell into the Whalympic Torch, which was supposed to burn throughout the Whalympics, so that was extremely unfortunate. And then the Whalympic Torch was knocked over and this started a fire at the side of the lagoon, which was one of the most unfortunate things that can happen at a major sporting event.

All the animals watching from the side of the lagoon started panicking, which was quite understandable. Fortunately, the art teacher didn't panic and realised very quickly that they needed to think of a way to put the fire out.

"Where's Wellington?" he asked loudly.

"I don't know," the PE teacher and the English teacher answered together, also quite loudly, though they didn't really know why the art teacher was asking where Wellington was.

Swimmy heard them, because they were talking quite loudly, and he didn't really know why the art teacher was asking where Wellington was either, but he thought he probably knew.

"I think I probably know," said Swimmy, quite loudly as well, because the fire was making everyone speak loudly for some reason.

"Well, please go and get him," said the art teacher,

"OK!" shouted Swimmy. And Swimmy swam off.

Wellington quickly forgot about being sad and cross and started to feel very surprised when he saw Swimmy swimming over to him. Not because it was unusual to see Swimmy swimming. Swimmy liked swimming and was a very good swimmer. It was surprising because Wellington thought the Whalympics were going on and he thought there was at least one more swimming forwards race for Swimmy to be taking part in.

"Wellington, come quickly, there's been an accident!" Swimmy cried.

As soon as Wellington heard there'd been an accident, he came quickly. He wanted to help. And as he was coming quickly, he smiled a little bit. Not because he was happy about the accident, but because he thought that if he wanted to come quickly and help when there'd been an accident, then he probably wasn't very selfish after all. And not being selfish made him happy.

PANIC

*I*t's normal to panic. Even though everyone knows you're not supposed to. Whenever anyone panics, they almost always hear someone saying 'Don't panic!' But they still panic. In fact, sometimes hearing someone saying 'Don't panic!' actually makes you panic. In fact, some people even say 'Don't panic!' when they themselves are panicking.

So everyone panics sometimes. Although they're not supposed to. Most people realise that if you don't panic then it's easier to stay calm and actually do something sensible. It's very difficult to do anything sensible if you're panicking. Particularly if people are yelling 'Don't panic!' at you. That's why you shouldn't panic.

The reason people do panic is because they need help. And when you need help, you can stay calm and ask somebody if they could please help. But by panicking you let them know very very quickly that you really really need help. Now! Which isn't always as clear when you stay calm.

And when you panic, you don't have to ask anybody in particular for help. You just panic and everyone who sees you will realise straight away that you really really need help. Now! That's the reason people panic.

The Whalympic Torch had been knocked over and some people had needed help and started panicking.

Then the fire had shot up and some more people had needed help and started panicking.

Then the fire had spread and started getting bigger and started jumping from tree to tree around the lagoon and nearly everyone was panicking by that point.

That was the situation that the art teacher had found himself in. However, he hadn't panicked. Because he wasn't just very good at organising things. He was also very good at staying calm and doing sensible things. Actually, that was one of the main reasons he was so good at organising things.

So the art teacher had stayed calm and looked at everyone panicking. And he had realised that they were panicking because they really really needed help. So he had tried to think who could really really help. And he had thought of Wellington.

Swimmy hadn't panicked either. He was quite good at staying calm, too. He was called Swimmy because he was good at swimming but he was actually quite good at lots of things besides swimming. He was quite good at painting, too. And he liked the art teacher. So he usually listened to what the art teacher said, which is why he'd heard the art teacher ask where Wellington was, as well as the fact that the art teacher had asked it quite loudly.

Wellington hadn't panicked either when Swimmy had shown up and asked him to come quickly to the lagoon. Wellington did panic sometimes but he'd been so excited about being able to help that he'd never even thought about panicking. So he'd just followed Swimmy quickly to the lagoon. Not as quickly as Swimmy could swim, but as quickly as Wellington could swim without starting to wobble.

When Wellington arrived at the lagoon, he didn't panic either. He had a look at what was going on and quickly made some connections. He saw quite a lot of fire and quite a lot of whales, and other animals, doing quite a lot of panicking. So he quickly made the connection that the whales and the other animals were panicking because of the fire.

Swimmy had actually told Wellington about the fire on their way to the lagoon but once he saw it for himself, it was even more obvious that the fire was the reason that the whales and the other animals were panicking. There was quite a lot of fire.

Swimmy had also told Wellington that the art teacher had asked him to fetch him, so Wellington looked at the art teacher and saw that he wasn't panicking. He seemed quite calm and smiled when he saw Wellington. Wellington quickly realised that if the art teacher was being calm, then he was probably doing something sensible and probably had a good reason for asking Swimmy to go and fetch him. And Wellington quickly realised that everyone panicking because of the fire probably really really needed help.

So he connected all that together and realised quite quickly that the art teacher thought that he, Wellington, would be able to help.

So Wellington thought how he, Wellington, might be able to help.

The problem – the cause of all the panic – was fire. And the best way of getting rid of fire was normally with the opposite of fire – which was water. So water would help get rid of the panic.

And one thing Wellington was very good
at – not the only thing he was very good
at but one thing he was probably better at
than all the other whales – was squirting
water in unusual ways. Normally he squirted
water in unusual ways to be exciting or to be
surprising. Or at least interesting. Here, he
would have to do it to be accurate and efficient.
Accurate and efficient would probably put
the fire out more quickly than unusual or
surprising, he thought. And, looking at them,
most of his potential audience didn't really
seem in the mood for an exciting or surprising
show anyway.

Having worked all that out, which had
actually only taken a few seconds, Wellington
got to work. He hadn't actually put out fire
before by squirting water at it but he knew
that if he sprayed water on the fire, it should
go out. He knew enough about opposites to
know that. And he decided that it would be
a good idea to start with the big bits of fire
first and then do the little bits of fire after. He

soon realised though that the little bits were growing and turning into bigger bits, so he did some scattering squirts at them. And some fire was quite big in a small place and some fire was quite small but spread over a bigger place. So for some fire he needed strong narrow jets and for some fire he needed weaker, but wider jets. Wellington quite enjoyed putting out the fire.

As he was putting out the fire, the other whales and the other animals saw what he was doing and started to stop panicking. Putting out a fire seemed like a much better way of stopping people panicking than yelling 'Don't panic!' at them.

So Wellington enjoyed doing it more and more. Some whales who had stopped panicking even started saying 'Wellington, Wellington, Wellington, Wellington', but not quietly and not to themselves. They were cheering it loudly, so everyone could hear it. And when Wellington heard it, it made him enjoy putting out the fire even more. And he started understanding better which kinds of squirt were needed for which kinds of fire, which was satisfying. And the bits of fire did actually start going out, which was relieving. If they'd just kept on growing and getting bigger, Wellington might even have started panicking himself. But they didn't, so he didn't.

After a few minutes, all the bits of fire had all been put out and everyone had stopped panicking.

Even the English teacher, who had really liked the idea of having the Whalympic Torch burn throughout the duration of the Whalympics, understood that it was better to put out all the bits of fire – even the Whalympic Torch – than to risk anything catching fire again.

The English teacher had actually been one of the whales who had panicked the most, so she was very happy and relieved when all the fires had been put out and she could stop shouting 'Don't panic!' at people, and get back to being sensible.

CELEBRATIONS

C elebrations are supposed to be happy
occasions. Normally, they are supposed
to be so happy that the word happy isn't
enough and people use lots of other words like
'jolly', 'joyful', 'jubilant' and even 'jovial'. The
word for the celebration doesn't have to begin
with 'j' – you can have a wonderful celebration
or a beautiful celebration, or, if you're not
trying to impress the English teacher, you can
quite happily have a happy celebration.

There had always been a celebration
planned for the end of the Whalympics. To
make it as fair as possible, the PE teacher,
the English teacher and the art teacher
had decided to include all the competition
participants equally, but let the ones who had

won medals wear the medals they had won.
The ones who had won medals had all already
had their medal ceremonies so they didn't need
another ceremony during the celebration. In
this way, the ones who hadn't won any medals
still wouldn't be able to wear any, but they
wouldn't get cross or accidentally start feeling
selfish. After all, the celebration was supposed
to be a joyful, jovial occasion, as the English
teacher said, and the PE teacher and the art
teacher agreed that it would be better if no one
was sad and everyone was happy.

And the celebration really was a jolly,
joyful, jubilant, jovial occasion. In fact, it even
had an extra added bit of jollity, joyfulness,
jubilance and joviality because everyone was
so relieved that the fire hadn't hurt anyone or
caused any major damage. After Wellington
had put out all the bits of fire and everyone
had been able to stop panicking, they had
been able to finish the synchronised breaching
competition. After that, they had held the
other three competitions that had still needed

holding as well.

Swimmy had taken part in the final competition of the Whalympics, which was another one where whales had to swim forwards quickly. He was good at those. But in this one, he had to do it in a team with three other whales. And although Swimmy had swum forwards very quickly at the start of the race, he had unfortunately dropped the chunk of wood he was supposed to give to the next whale on his team. And you weren't supposed to drop the chunk of wood.

That had been a little disappointing when it had happened but Swimmy didn't mind too much afterwards. He still had two gold medals from the races he had won and the other whales on his team didn't seem to mind too much either. They realised that the chunk of wood had been very slippery and that it's easy to drop slippery things. And Swimmy, just like the other whales on his team and everyone else, was generally very happy that the fires had been put out. In fact, Swimmy was even a little bit happier than everyone else because he'd helped by managing not to panic and by swimming off to get Wellington. Helping usually makes someone happy.

Happiest of all was Wellington. There were lots of reasons for Wellington to be happy. Firstly, he was happy because the celebration was so joyous. Secondly, he was happy because the fire had been put out and everyone was safe. Thirdly, he was happy because he had been the whale to help put out the fire. Finally, or finally for now anyway, Wellington was happy because he originally hadn't expected to be very happy at all during the celebration.

When he'd left the Whalympics and swum off on his own, he had thought a bit about the celebration. And when he was thinking a bit, he had expected all the whales who had won medals in the competitions to be happily wearing their medals. As he wasn't taking part in any of the competitions, he knew he wasn't going to win any medals. So he knew he wasn't going to be wearing a medal. And he wasn't wearing a medal. But somehow, that didn't matter anymore.

Wellington was just thinking about what a nice surprise it was being happy at the celebration when he had another surprise. And this was a nice surprise, too.

The art teacher, who really had organised the Whalympics very well, had had the idea of making a few spare medals. They'd needed 138 medals but the art teacher had suggested making 150. "Just in case," he'd said. He'd organised lots of things before and had learned that it was often good to have spares of things just in case. If you had things just in case, the case didn't always come up, but if you didn't prepare any spares, then you often seemed to end up in the case where you wished you'd prepared some.

So they'd made 12 spare medals: 4 gold, 4 silver and 4 bronze. They'd used one of the spare bronze medals already, because there had been one race in which two whales had actually come third. So when that happened,

the art teacher was pleased to have prepared
some spares just in case something like that
had happened.

No-one, not even the art teacher, had
really expected the fire to happen. But the
art teacher did realise, after the fire had
happened and after Wellington had put it out,
that this was another case where they could
use one of the spare medals.

During the celebration, the art teacher
called for everyone to be quiet, which was a bit
unusual because happy occasions are usually
loud, but everyone understood why he wanted
everyone to be quiet when he said it was
because he had an announcement to make.
It's much easier to make announcements when
everyone's started being quiet than when
everyone's still being loud.

After everyone had quietened down, he
made his announcement, which was asking
Wellington to come to the podium where they'd
held the medal ceremonies earlier. Wellington
was usually quite good at making connections

but he wasn't really expecting to have to make any connections at that moment, so he just swam over to the podium without really having any idea what was going on.

When the art teacher presented him with a gold medal for being the best at putting out fires, Wellington finally, and very surprisingly, felt like he really was the star of the Whalympics after all. Even though he had been quite sure that that was something that really wasn't going to happen.

As the celebration continued and Wellington saw lots of other whales wearing their medals for winning or coming second or coming third in the competitions, Wellington remembered that lots of the other whales were also the stars of the Whalympics. Realising this didn't make Wellington any less happy. He liked realising things. In fact, he liked the fact that there were lots of stars of the Whalympics, and that he was one of them.

The celebration lasted longer than a normal school day but it still finished at some point.

Even the most jovial celebrations have to finish at some point. So when that point came, Wellington said 'goodbye' to everyone and swam home, wearing his medal.

As he swam home, he thought about how happy it made him that there were lots of stars of the Whalympics, and that he was one of them.

HOME

Wellington's dad was at home, waiting for Wellington to come home after the Whalympics. He knew the celebration was supposed to last a bit longer than a normal school day, so he wasn't too surprised that Wellington hadn't come home at the normal home time. Though he wouldn't have been too surprised if Wellington had come home at the normal home time because he wasn't sure if Wellington would want to take part in the celebration. He wasn't really sure in general how Wellington really felt about the Whalympics and whether Wellington was going to enjoy it or not.

Over the last few weeks, Wellington's dad hadn't really spoken to Wellington very much about the Whalympics. He had realised that there was going to be a day of competitions and he had realised quite quickly that Wellington probably wasn't going to be taking part in any of the competitions. He knew that Wellington wobbled a bit when he tried to swim fast because his tail looked a bit like a wellington boot.

Wellington's dad had been happy when Wellington had told him that he'd won the name comp. And he'd been happy when Wellington had told him that he was going to be doing the opening ceremony. Wellington had even asked his dad if he'd be able to come and watch the opening ceremony. His dad had said that he was afraid he'd have to work. His dad almost always had to work while Wellington was at school. Because he had to spend his time when Wellington wasn't at school looking after Wellington. Three year-old whales are already quite big but it's still nice to have a grown-up to look after them. So that only left the time when Wellington was at school for his dad to work. But he always made sure he'd finished work and was at home ready to look after Wellington by the time Wellington got home from school.

Wellington's dad was waiting at home. He'd got some krill and ketchup ready. He'd thought that if Wellington hadn't really enjoyed the Whalympics then he'd at least be happy to have some krill and ketchup for dinner. And if Wellington had enjoyed the Whalympics, then he still wouldn't mind eating some krill and ketchup for dinner. Wellington liked krill and ketchup. His dad knew that.

When Wellington came home, his dad was a bit anxious about asking how he was, so he just said,

"Hi, Wellington, I've got some krill and ketchup ready."

Wellington's dad had actually thought for a long time about what to say when Wellington came home. He'd started thinking just before normal home time and only stopped thinking just before Wellington had come in. 'I've got

some krill and ketchup ready' sounded like
something that couldn't possibly make anyone
unhappy. Certainly not Wellington. Wellington
liked krill and ketchup. His dad knew that.

When Wellington came home and his dad
said that he'd got some krill and ketchup
ready, Wellington certainly wasn't unhappy.
He seemed quite the opposite of unhappy.
Happy – even joyous or even delighted. His
dad wasn't sure if Wellington was this happy
just because of the krill and ketchup or if he
was already happy because he'd enjoyed the
Whalympics. He was still a bit anxious about
asking, so he was relieved when Wellington
started talking, because it meant he didn't
have to.

And after Wellington had started talking,
Wellington kept on talking. And talking.
And talking. So Wellington's dad hardly had
to say anything at all for a long time, and
he soon stopped being anxious. Wellington
told him all about the opening ceremony,
about how the bits that were supposed to be

expected had been expected and how the bits that were supposed to be surprising had been surprising. He told him about his tricks with the Whalympic Rings and the Whalympic Torch, though he didn't say anything about poetry or geometry because he hadn't really been thinking about them.

And then he told his dad about the competitions, how he'd seen Swimmy win a gold medal. And then about how he'd started feeling cross and unhappy and about how he'd swum off. And then about how Swimmy had come to fetch him and about the fire and about how he'd put out the fire and about the celebration and about how he'd got a medal and about how there'd been lots of stars of the Whalympics and about how he'd been one of them.

While Wellington was telling his dad all this, his dad hadn't really had to say anything other than 'Oh', 'Wow', 'Really?' and other things like that which helped to show Wellington that he was still listening. And as he had still been listening, it hadn't been very difficult at all to say these things.

Wellington didn't mind that his dad wasn't saying very much. He was enjoying telling him all about everything and his dad was making it quite clear that he was still listening. And he saw that his dad must have been quite happy, or quite tired, or quite sad, or quite surprised, or maybe all of that at the same time, because he saw, as he was telling him about everything, how small tears were trickling down his dad's face. He saw how his dad was crying.

After Wellington had finished telling his dad all about everything, and after he'd finished his krill and ketchup, which had been very nice, Wellington got ready for bed.

When he was ready, he swam over to his dad and said,

"It's been a great day. Goodnight, Dad."

And his dad said,

"Yes it has. Goodnight. I love you, Oslo."

Normally, when people called him 'Oslo', Wellington said 'Wellington' straight away. And this time, Wellington was just about to say 'Wellington', but he didn't. He was just so happy, and maybe he was quite tired as well. In fact, he didn't even think about saying 'Wellington'. Maybe he didn't even really realise that his dad hadn't called him 'Wellington'. Whether he did or not, he didn't say 'Wellington'. He just smiled and said,

"I love you too, Dad."

And Wellington went to bed. And Wellington was happy.